ISBN 978-0-06-171486-3

Typography by Jeanne L. Hogle
Printed at RR Donnelley
Reynosa, Tamaulipas, Mexico
April 2010

By the #1 *New York Times* Bestselling Author

John Grogan

Marley and the Kittens

illustrated by Richard Cowdrey

HARPER
An Imprint of HarperCollinsPublishers

The little red car chugged down the road on
a warm summer's day. Mommy and Daddy and
Cassie and Baby Louie were on their way home
from a picnic in the country. And in the backseat,
with his head stuck out the window, was their big
yellow puppy, Marley.

All of a sudden, Marley began to bark and yelp and
whine. He looked like he might leap right out the window.
"What is it, boy?" Cassie asked.
"Aroof! Woof! Woof!" Marley said.
"Waddy need potty!" Baby Louie said.

Daddy stopped the car, and out jumped Marley.
But he did not poop and he did not pee. What he did
was sniff his way along the side of the road, dragging
Mommy behind him. His tail wagged wildly as he
snorted and snuffed through the weeds like a vacuum
cleaner. When he finally stopped, Mommy called out,

"Oh my goodness! Look what Marley found!"
"They're so cute!" Cassie exclaimed.
"Yeow-yow!" Baby Louie shrieked.

In the weeds lay two tiny, fluffy kittens. "They're just little babies," Mommy said.

"And they don't have a mama," added Cassie.

Marley nuzzled their bellies with his nose and whined.

"Don't worry, Big Guy," Daddy said. "We're not going to leave them here by the side of the road."

Cassie cuddled one kitten and Baby Louie the other.

"I'm naming mine Lucky," Cassie said.

"Mine Yow-Yow," Baby Louie declared.

"It looks like our family just got bigger,"
Mommy said.

Back at the house, Lucky and Yow-Yow made themselves
at home. They rubbed against the cupboards and sniffed the
floor. *This calls for my super-duper doggie welcome,* Marley
thought as he raced in from the garage, sliding across the tile
and not stopping until he rammed the trash can.

"Settle down, Marley!" Mommy scolded. "You'll scare the
kittens!"

Cassie placed a bowl of water and a plate of tuna fish on the floor and called, "Here, kitty, kitty, kitties. Time to eat!" The kittens came running—and so did Marley.

Oh boy! Treats!

"That's for the kittens, not you!" Cassie yelled.

"Bad dog, Marley!" Daddy said.

"Baa boo boo, Waddy!" Baby Louie repeated.

After lunch, Lucky and Yow-Yow cleaned
their faces with their tongues and paws.

Marley cleaned his face, too.
"Marley, no!" Mommy yelled.
"Yuck yuck!" Baby Louie cried.

The kittens played with the cords from
the window blinds. They pounced and
tugged and batted them back and forth.
"Oh, how adorable," Mommy cooed.

But when Marley joined the fun, Mommy stopped smiling. "No, Marley! You're wrecking everything!"

The kittens hopped onto the kitchen counter and tiptoed among the jars and glasses. "Look how graceful they are," Daddy marveled.

Then came Marley. "Arf! Arf!" he barked, as if to say, *Wait for me!* He leaped onto a chair and then up onto the counter to join his new friends. But Marley was no graceful kitten. "Bad dog, Marley!"

The kittens discovered their brand-new litter box.

Marley discovered it, too.

"No wee wee, Waddy!" Baby Louie yelled.

Mommy opened a kitchen drawer for a towel, and when she looked back the kittens had climbed in. They curled up and fell fast asleep. "Aren't they precious?" Mommy said. "So cute!" Cassie agreed.

Marley wanted to be precious and cute just like the kittens.
But when he tried the same trick, no one found it either.

Daddy moved the litter box out to the garage and installed a tiny cat door so the kittens could come and go whenever they liked. *Great idea!* Marley thought, and tried to use the new door, too.

"You're in time-out, mister!" Mommy ordered.
What did I do this time? Marley wondered.
He just wanted to be loved like the kittens.
He wanted to be popular like them, too. But the
more he tried, the more he messed up. *Stupid cats,*
he thought. *They're so perfect. PURRRRR-fect. And
I'm just a dog. A dog that can't do anything right.
Sometimes I wish I'd never found those kittens.*

As Marley sat there pouting, he felt something brush against him. There were Lucky and Yow-Yow. They rubbed their whiskers against his sides and purred loudly, stretching their faces up toward his. Marley forgot all about being sad. *You came to keep me company!*

"Hey, everyone, come look," Cassie shouted.
"The kittens have put themselves in time-out!"
"I guess they missed their new pal," Daddy said,
grinning. Even Mommy had to laugh. "Like three
peas in a pod," she marveled.

"Oh, Marley," Cassie said, giving him a hug. "See how popular you are."

"The kittens sure are cute, but they could never take your place," Daddy added, scratching him behind the ears. "There'll always be only one Marley."

"We love you just the way you are," Mommy said.

"Waddy, you wock!" Baby Louie screeched. And the whole family laughed.

Marley pranced and danced and wiggled and squiggled from tongue to tail. He would never be a cute kitten, and that was all right. He was Marley, one of a kind. No apologies needed.

Friends forever.